PENGUIN WORKSHOP
An Imprint of Penguin Random House LLC, New York

Visit us online at www.penguinrandomhouse.com.

Library of Congress Cataloging-in-Publication Data is available upon request.

ISBN 9781524787042   10 9 8 7 6 5 4 3 2 1

www.jessicahische.is/writing

for

Ramona, Charlie, and George

You inspire me to be my best today, tomorrow, and every day.

TOMORROW
I'LL BE
Kind

Words and pictures by

JESSICA HISCHE

Penguin Workshop

Tomorrow I'll be

Lift

when I see someone **in need**

I won't stand by or hesitate,

I'll **get up** and take the **lead**!

Tomorrow I'll be

Your turn—I'll **wait** for you

And when I'm stuck, **I won't give up**.

I'll take **time** to see it through.

Tomorrow I'll be

to creatures **big** and **small**

Thinking of what others need—

I'll show **tenderness** to all.

Tomorrow I'll be

To myself I will be **true**

And **prove** that you can **trust** in me
through all I **say** and **do**.

and show you how I care

We all have ways of **giving back** and **gifts** that we can **share**.

Tomorrow I'll be

GRA

for what you've **given** me

Appreciating all I **have**—your **love**, especially.

My **heart**, my guiding light

The smallest spark of **kindness**
shines through the darkest night.

Tomorrow I'll be all the things I **strive** to be each day . . .

Helpful PATIENT Gentle HONEST

and even when it's difficult, I'll **work** to find a way.

But **tonight** I'm very sleepy,
so now it's time to **rest**.

I'll **dream** of all the good that comes
when we all just **try our best**.